Marv and the Monkey

Written by Tom Ottway
Illustrated by Iole E Rosa

Collins

Who's in this story?

Listen and say 🎧1

Download the audio at www.collins.co.uk/839645

Carlo
Marv
Tony

2 My name is Tony, but this is a story about Marv. He lives in a different country, but he came to visit me last week.

I live in a big city. My parents and my big brother Carlo work at the flower market. Marv lives in a small village. He sent me a picture of him and his house.

Marv is my penfriend! He writes letters to me, and I write letters to him.

Hi Marv,
How are you?
I can't wait to see
you next week...

Most people use email but Marv and I like writing letters. We write in English.

Hi Tony!
How are you?
I'm very happy.
See you on Friday
at the airport!...

On Friday, Dad and I met Marv at the airport.

"Wow! This city is so big!" said Marv.

He took a photo on his phone. It's a red phone. Very cool!

"Would you like to visit the market, Marv?" I asked.

"Oh yes, please! Can I take my phone?" said Marv.

"Yes!" I said.

"But be careful!" said Carlo.

At my parents' flower stall, Marv took lots of photos of the different flowers. Then he saw the monkeys.

"Look! A baby monkey," said Marv. "I love it!"

The monkeys jumped and climbed on us.

But then ...

I can't find my phone.

The baby monkey ran. It ran over a music stall. It had a red thing in its hand!

“Oh, no! The monkey’s got my phone!” said Marv.

Stop that monkey!

We ran after the monkey.
“Where did it go?” I said.

Oh no! The monkey was on a food stall.
The man on the stall was not happy.
“My spices!” he said. “Stop that monkey!”

“Oh no! Where is it going?” asked Marv.

“I think it’s going to the kitchen stall.” I said.

We all ran. Me, Marv, Carlo and the food stall holder.

But the monkey ran faster! And then it jumped! ... over the plates ... over the cups ... And into the pans!

The baby monkey dropped the phone.

The kitchen stall holder was not happy.

"Wait ... This is a toy phone!" said Marv.

"Look! *Your* phone is in your pocket!" said Carlo.

"The monkey didn't take your phone," I said.

"I'm sorry," said Marv to the monkey, "You're only a baby and you wanted a toy."

So Carlo bought a banana.
He gave it to Marv.

"For the monkey," he said.

Thank you for a
fantastic holiday.
Here's a photo!

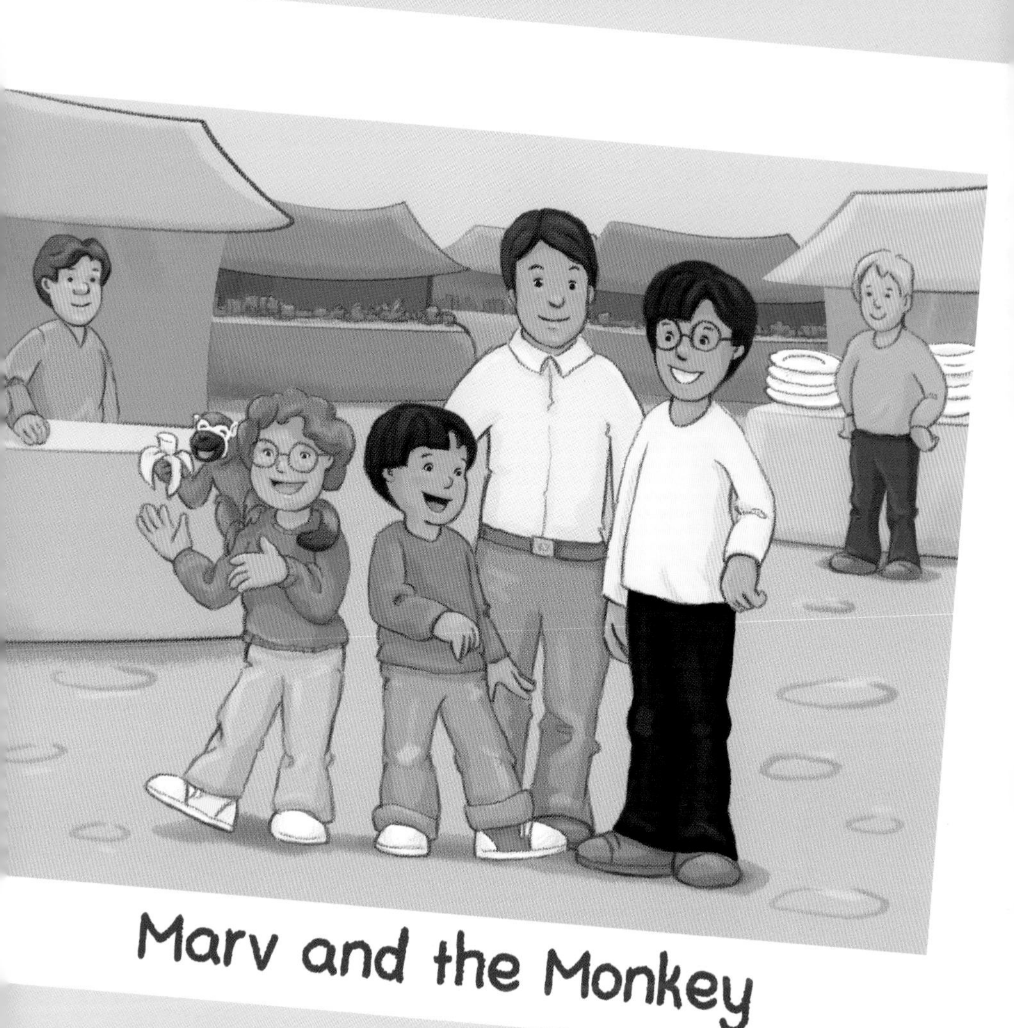

Marv and the Monkey

Everyone was happy! Marv had his phone.
The monkey had a banana! And Marv had
a fantastic holiday.

Picture dictionary

Listen and repeat 

1 Look and order the story

2 Listen and say  

Collins

Published by Collins
An imprint of HarperCollins*Publishers*
Westerhill Road
Bishopbriggs
Glasgow
G64 2QT

HarperCollins*Publishers*
1st Floor, Watermarque Building
Ringsend Road
Dublin 4
Ireland

William Collins' dream of knowledge for all began with the publication of his first book in 1819.

A self-educated mill worker, he not only enriched millions of lives, but also founded a flourishing publishing house. Today, staying true to this spirit, Collins books are packed with inspiration, innovation and practical expertise. They place you at the centre of a world of possibility and give you exactly what you need to explore it.

10 9 8 7 6 5 4 3 2

ISBN 978-0-00-839645-9

www.collins.co.uk/elt

British Library Cataloguing in Publication Data

A catalogue record for this publication is available from the British Library.

Author: Tom Ottway
Illustrator: Iole E Rosa (Beehive)
Series editor: Rebecca Adlard
Commissioning editor: Zoë Clarke
Publishing manager: Lisa Todd
Product managers: Jennifer Hall and Caroline Green
In-house editor: Alma Puts Keren
Project manager: Emily Hooton
Editor: Frances Amrani
Proofreaders: Natalie Murray and Michael Lamb
Cover designer: Kevin Robbins
Typesetter: 2Hoots Publishing Services Ltd
Audio produced by id audio, London
Reading guide author: Emma Wilkinson
Production controller: Rachel Weaver
Printed and bound by: GPS Group, Slovenia

MIX
Paper from responsible sources
FSC C007454

This book is produced from independently certified FSC™ paper to ensure responsible forest management.

For more information visit: **www.harpercollins.co.uk/green**

Download the audio for this book and a reading guide for parents and teachers at www.collins.co.uk/839645